This book
belongs to

_____

Mad About Munsch!

Mad About Munsch!

A Robert Munsch Collection

Illustrated by

Michael Martchenko

and

The children of Sir Isaac Brock Public School

Scholastic Canada Ltd.
Toronto New York London Auckland Sydney
Mexico City New Delhi Hong Kong Buenos Aires

Library and Archives Canada Cataloguing in Publication
Munsch, Robert N., 1945-
Mad about Munsch! : a Robert Munsch collection / illustrated
by Michael Martchenko and the students of Sir Isaac Brock
Public School.

Contents: More pies -- Zoom -- Smelly socks -- Boo! -- The
sandcastle contest -- Braids.
ISBN 978-1-4431-0239-1

1. Children's stories, Canadian (English). I. Martchenko,
Michael II. Sir Isaac Brock Public School III. Title.

PS8576.U575M849 2010   jC813'.54   C2010-901936-9

www.scholastic.ca

6 5 4 3 2 1   Printed in Singapore 46   10 11 12 13 14

Contents

For Samuel Or,
Vancouver, British Columbia.
— R.M.

More Pies!

by Robert Munsch

Illustrated by Michael Martchenko

Samuel woke up really hungry.

He went downstairs and ate a bowl of cereal:

Chuka - chuka - chuka - chuka - chuka - chuka - CHOMP!

Then he said, "Mom, can I please have some more?"

"Yes," said his mom. "You are a growing boy and you need to eat."

So Samuel's mom gave him another bowl of cereal, two milk shakes, and a stack of pancakes. Samuel ate it all really fast:

Chuka - chuka - chuka - chuka - chuka - chuka - CHOMP!

Then Samuel said, "I am still hungry. Could I please have some more?"

"Yes," said his mom. "But I think this will be enough."

So Samuel's mom got out a really big salad bowl, filled it full of cereal, and gave him two milk shakes, three stacks of pancakes, and a fried chicken. Samuel ate it all really fast:

Chuka - chuka - chuka - chuka - chuka - chuka - CHOMP!

Then Samuel said, "I am still really hungry. Could I please have seven fried chickens?"

"Seven fried chickens!" yelled his mom. "Enough is enough! Nothing more to eat until lunch! Go out and play."

Samuel went outside and rolled around in the grass yelling,

"Staaaaarving
    Staaaaarving!
        HELP!
            I'm starving!"

Samuel's little brother came running outside. He said, "Samuel, if you are so hungry, why don't you go to the pie-eating contest? There is one at the fair in the park."

So Samuel got on the bus and
went to the park.

Samuel walked right into the middle of the pie-eating contest and said, "Give me pies."

A judge looked at Samuel and said, "You are just a little kid! Go home."

A fireman, a lumberjack, and a construction worker were sitting at a long table. The construction worker said, "It won't hurt to let this little kid eat a pie."

So Samuel climbed on a chair
and the judge gave everybody one
blueberry pie.

The judge yelled, "One, two, three, eat!"
and they all ate their pies really fast:

Chuka - chuka - chuka -
chuka - chuka - chuka -
CHOMP!

When they were done, the lumberjack said, "Oh, my tummy hurts." He turned purple and fell under the table.

The judge said, "Samuel, that was excellent eating, but surely you are done! You are just a little kid."

Samuel said, "I am not starving anymore, but more pies still sounds like a good idea."

So the judge gave everybody two peach pies. He yelled, "One, two, three, eat!" and they all ate their pies really fast:

Chuka - chuka - chuka - chuka - chuka - chuka - CHOMP!

When they were done, the fireman said, "Oh, my tummy hurts." He turned green and fell under the table.

The judge said, "I don't believe this!"
He gave Samuel and the construction
worker each three cherry pies.
He yelled, "One, two, three, eat!"
and they ate their pies really fast:

Chuka - chuka - chuka -
chuka - chuka - chuka - CHOMP!

When they were done, the construction worker said, "Oh, my tummy hurts." He turned blue and fell under the table.

"Amazing!" said the judge. "Samuel wins first prize! Samuel wins the PRIZE PIE!"

Samuel took his prize pie, got on the bus, and went back home . . .

for lunch. When he walked into the kitchen, his mom said, "Samuel, I know you are really hungry, so I made you pies for lunch."

"Pies?" said Samuel. "Ahhhhh — my tummy hurts." He turned green and fell under the table.

But Samuel's little brother said, "YUM! PIES!" and ate the pies really fast:

Chuka -chuka - chuka - chuka - chuka - chuka - CHOMP!

More Pies!

More Pies! started as a lunchtime story in 1973 at the Bay Area Childcare Center in Coos Bay, Oregon. I had no idea that it would ever be a book. It was just a funny story to tell before lunch. Unlike a lot of my stories, the character in it was not a real kid. This was a problem when, years later, I decided to make it into a book. I had no picture of Samuel to send to Michael Martchenko.

I could have used a kid I knew, but it seemed to me that after twenty-seven years of being a Samuel story, it was too late to change it. So I decided to wait until a Samuel wrote me a fan letter. Since I get about ten thousand letters a year, I knew that one would write eventually, and one finally did, after I had waited only four months.

The Samuel wrote me an excellent letter. I had no idea what he looked like, but I wrote back and asked if he wanted to be in a book. He did. So Samuel sent me pictures of his family and his house. Then the story changed because of Samuel's pictures, and Samuel's little brother ended up being in the story along with Samuel.

I know this is a strange way to write a book, but it works for me!

— R.M.

*For Lauretta Reid,
Orillia, Ontario.
— R.M.*

ZOOM!

by Robert Munsch

Illustrated by Michael Martchenko

When her mother came to pick her up at school, Lauretta said, "Look at this ratty old wheelchair! I've had it since forever. I need a new wheelchair!"

"Guess what?" said her mother. "We are getting one today! I wanted it to be a surprise!"

So they went to the wheelchair
store to get a nice new wheelchair.

Lauretta's mother said, "How about this? Look at this! A nice new five-speed wheelchair."

Lauretta rode the wheelchair around the store:

ZOOOOOM

ZOOOOOM

ZOOOOOM

and said, "Too slow."

Then Lauretta's mother said, "Well, how about this? Look at this! A nice new ten-speed wheelchair."

Lauretta rode the wheelchair around the store:

ZOOOOOOOOOOM

ZOOOOOOOOOOOM

ZOOOOOOOOOOOOM

and said, "Too slow."

Then Lauretta's mother said, "Well, how about this? Look at this! A nice new 15-speed wheelchair. It's fantastic. It's purple, green, and yellow. It costs lots and lots of money."

Lauretta rode the wheelchair around the store really fast:

ZOOOOOOOOOOOOOOM

ZOOOOOOOOOOOOOOOM

ZOOOOOOOOOOOOOOOM

and said, "Too slow."

Her mother said, "Well, what sort of wheelchair do you want?"

Lauretta went way in the back of the store and said, "This is what I want. A nice new 92-speed, black, silver, and red, dirt-bike wheelchair."

"Oh, no," said her mother. "It costs *toooo* much money. It goes *toooo* fast. You are *toooo* little for a wheelchair like that."

The lady from the store came over and said, "Take it home for a day. Give it a try for free! See if you like it."

"Wow!" said Lauretta. "We can try it for a day and it will not even cost any money! Pleeeeeeease!"

"Oh, all right," said her mother.

When they got home, Lauretta put the wheelchair in first gear and rode up and down the driveway:

ZOOM

But first gear was very slow. So she put it in tenth gear and went:

ZOOOOOOOOOM

That was still too slow, so she put it into twentieth gear and went really fast:

ZOOOOOOOOOOOOOOOOOOOM

and crashed into her brother.

He said, "Lauretta, if you are going to go so fast, don't go on the driveway. Go on the road."

"Okay, okay, okay!" said Lauretta. "I'll go on the road."

Lauretta went out to the road, put
her wheelchair into ninety-second
gear and went:

ZOOOOOOOOOOOOOOOOOOOOOOOOM

as fast as she could.

A police car came up beside Lauretta. The police officer rolled down the window and yelled, "Hey, kid, pull over! You're speeding."

Lauretta pulled over and the police officer gave her a 100-dollar ticket for speeding. He tied it right to her wrist. Then he said, "Go home, kid! You shouldn't even be on the road at all."

Lauretta went home saying, "Oh, I'm in trouble. Oh, I'm in trouble. Oh, I'm in trouble."

When she got home, her mother said, "Why, Lauretta, what's that on your wrist?"

"It's a ticket," said Lauretta.

"Oh," said her mother. "Is it a ticket to a movie?"

"No," said Lauretta.

"Is it a ticket to a hockey game?"

"No," said Lauretta.

"Is it a ticket to a baseball game?"

"No," said Lauretta. "It's a 100-dollar speeding ticket for speeding in my wheelchair."

"Oh, no!" said her mother. "This is terrible. What will your father say? What will your grandmother say? What will the neighbours say?"

(You know how mothers do that? Well, she did it for a long, long time.)

Finally it was dinnertime.

Lauretta's father said, "That wheelchair is too fast. We are going to have to take it back."

"Yes," said Lauretta's mother. "That wheelchair is too fast. We are going to have to take it back."

Meanwhile, Lauretta's older brother was trying to talk on the phone, argue with Lauretta, feed the dog, and use his fork all at the same time. He stuck the fork right through his finger.

Lauretta's mother yelled, "BLOOD!"

Lauretta's father yelled, "BLOOD!"

Lauretta said, "This house is going crazy."

They all ran out to the car. Lauretta's father turned the key, but the car wouldn't start.

"Oh, no!" yelled Lauretta's mother. "How are we going to get him to the hospital?"

"Don't worry," said Lauretta. "I'll take him in my wheelchair!"

She pulled her brother onto her lap and went down the street in ninety-second gear:

ZOOOOOOOOOOOOOOOOOOOOOOOOM

as fast as she could go.

That same police car came up
beside her.
   Lauretta pointed at her brother
and yelled, "BLOOOOOOD!"

So the police car went with Lauretta all the way to the hospital. Lauretta drove in and gave her brother to the doctor, and the doctor sewed up her brother's finger.

Then they went all the way home and knocked on the door:

BLAM, BLAM, BLAM, BLAM

Her mother said, "Oh, Lauretta, you saved your brother!"

Her father said, "You saved your brother! You couldn't have done it without your wheelchair. Lauretta, you can keep the wheelchair."

"Well," said Lauretta, "thank you very much. It's a very nice wheelchair, but I don't want that wheelchair anymore."

"Oh, no," said her mother.

"Oh, no," said her father. "What's the matter with the wheelchair?"

"Well," said Lauretta, "it's

TOO SLOW."

ZOOM!

In 1987 I was telling stories in Calgary and a kid named Grant stuck up his hand and said that he liked bicycles, so I made up a bicycle story. In the story Grant bought a bicycle that was so fast that he ended up getting a speeding ticket. It turned out to be a good story and I kept telling it. I could use it for anything that had wheels and some things that did not, like pogo sticks and skis. It also worked for wheelchairs, and I began using it whenever there was a kid in the audience who had a wheelchair.

Then, in 1997, a girl named Lauretta wrote and asked me for a story about a girl who walks with crutches and uses a wheelchair. Lauretta's mom sent along a note saying that Lauretta was born with spina bifida and hydrocephalus and scoliosis and used crutches for short distances and a wheelchair for longer trips. I sent Lauretta a copy of the story and later met her at one of my concerts. I decided to make the "bicycle or skateboard or wheelchair or ski or surfboard or car or rocket or canoe" story into a wheelchair book.

Now there was a problem. What about Grant? I wrote him and said that I wanted to change the bicycle story into a wheelchair story for a kid who used a wheelchair. He said that it was OK. Maybe the fact that he was twenty years old by then helped him to make his decision.

— R.M.

To Tina Fabian,
Hay River Dene Reserve,
Katlodeeche First Nation.
— R.M.

SMELLY SOCKS

Robert Munsch
Michael Martchenko

When Tina wanted new socks, her mom took her to the only store in town.

"This store only has black socks," said Tina. "Can we please go across the river and get some really good socks?"

"We can't drive right across the river because there is no bridge here," said Tina's mom. "You know it is a long, long, long way to the only bridge and besides, we don't have a car!"

So Tina went to her grandfather and said, "Can you please take me across the river in your boat? I want to buy some really good socks."

"The motor is not working on the boat," said her grandfather.

"Row!" said Tina. "We can row! I will row and you can sit in the back of the boat."

"You will row?" said her grandfather.

"YES!" said Tina. "Rowing is easy."

So Tina got in the boat and rowed slowly

SPLASH **SPLASH** **SPLASH.**

and the boat went in slow circles

SWISH! *SWISH!* *SWISH!*

Tina rowed fast

SPLASH **SPLASH** **SPLASH** **SPLASH** **SPLASH.**

and the boat went in fast circles

SWISH SWISH SWISH SWISH SWISH!

"This boat has forgotten how to row," said Tina.

"You sit in the back and tell me what to do," said her grandfather.

So Tina sat in the back and told her grandfather how to row, and her grandfather rowed all the way across the river. Then they walked all the way through the town to the big sock store.

At the store Tina tried on socks that were too big, socks that were too little, socks that were too blue, and socks that were too pink.

Tina tried on millions and millions of socks.

Finally she found a perfect pair of red, yellow, and green socks.

Then, since it was almost time for dinner, Tina and her grandfather ran back to the boat, and this time the boat sort of remembered how to row. Tina rowed round and round and round, and still got to the other side.

When they got back, Tina ran home and yelled, "Socks! Socks! Wonderful socks! These are the best socks I have ever seen in my life. Grandpa rowed me all the way across the river to get these socks. I am NEVER going to take them off."

"Never?" said Tina's mother.

"NNNNNNNNEVER!" said Tina.

"Uh-oh!" said Tina's mother.

So Tina wore her socks for a long time. She wore them for one, two, three, four, five, six, seven, eight, nine, ten whole days.

Her mother said, "Tina, I know you love these socks. Just let me wash them really quick. They will start to SMELL if you don't get them washed."

"Socks! Socks! Wonderful socks!" said Tina. "I am NEVER, NEVER going to take them off."

After Tina wore her socks for ten more days, the kids at school said, "Tina! What a smell! Change your socks."

"Socks! Wonderful socks!" said Tina. "I am NEVER, NEVER, NEVER, NEVER, NEVER going to take them off."

After Tina wore her socks for ten more days, a whole flock of Canada geese flew over her house and dropped right out of the sky from the smell.

Two moose walked through her yard and fell over from the smell.

Ducks, raccoons, and squirrels fell over when she walked to school.

Finally, even a skunk fell over from the smell.

Tina's friends decided to do something. They all came to her house and knocked on the door.

BLAM BLAM BLAM BLAM BLAM!

When Tina opened the door, they grabbed her and carried her to the river. Then they held their noses and took off her socks.

Some of the kids held Tina, and some
of the kids washed the socks.

SCRUB SCRUB SCRUB
SCRUB SCRUB!

All the fish in the river floated up to
the top and acted like they were dead.

The kids washed some more:

SCRUB SCRUB SCRUB
SCRUB SCRUB!

All the beavers ran out of the river and went to live with Tina's grandfather.
They washed some more:

SCRUB SCRUB SCRUB
SCRUB SCRUB!

Far down the river, people said, "How come the river smells like dirty socks?"

Finally the socks were clean.

"Wow!" said Tina. "They look nicer when they are clean."

"Wow!" said Tina. "They smell nicer when they are clean."

"Wow!" said Tina. "They feel nicer when they are clean."

Tina put on the socks and said, "I am going to wear clean socks from now on."

The beavers left her grandfather's house and went back into the river.

The Canada geese got up off the ground and flew away.

The fish decided that they were not dead after all, and jumped and splashed in the river.

Tina went to her mom and said, "My socks are nice and clean, and I think it would be very nice if you took me to town to get me a nice new red, yellow, and green shirt."

"Promise to wash it?" said her mom.

"No," said Tina. "If I wait long enough, the kids at school will wash it for me."

SMELLY SOCKS

In November of 1984, I was telling stories at the Dene reserve across the river from Hay River, Northwest Territories. I could see the reserve from Hay River, but I had to drive a long way to get to a bridge.

Only three kids came. I was really glad that anyone showed up and I told a new story about each kid. Tina, one of the kids, had very colourful socks, and I made up a story where she kept switching her dirty socks for other people's clean socks. It was not very good, but Tina liked it.

The dirty socks idea turned out to be a good one, and I kept telling sock stories. After about five years the story settled down, got good, and became one of my regular telling stories. Then in 2003 my editor said "Hey! Let's do the sock story."

By then Tina was grown up, had a baby, and was going to school in Fort Smith. She was not a little kid any more, but she was really happy that *Smelly Socks* was finally going to be a book.

— R.M.

For Lance,
Hamilton, Ontario.
— R.M.

On Halloween, Lance went to his father and said, "This year, I am not going to wear a mask. I'm going to paint my face and make it very, very scary."

"That's nice, Lance," said his father. "It's a lot less work for me. You go and paint your face."

So Lance went to the bathroom and
painted:

worms coming out of his hair,
ants crawling on his cheeks,
and snakes coming out of his mouth.

Then he went downstairs, walked up
behind his father, and said, "Boo!"

His father turned around and yelled,

"Ahhhhhhhhhhh!"

"Not scary enough!" said Lance.
"I wanted him to fall over."

So Lance went back upstairs and painted:
green brains coming out the side of his head,
one eye falling down over his face,
and orange goop coming out of his nose.
Then he went downstairs, walked up behind
his father, and said, "Boo!"
His father yelled,

"Ahhhhhhhhhhhh!"

and fell right over.
"Scary enough!" said Lance.

Then Lance put a pillowcase over his head, got another pillowcase for candy, and walked down the street.

He went up to a house:

KNOCK KNOCK KNOCK.

A big man opened the door and said, "First kid for Halloween! So nice to see a little kid for Halloween."

Lance lifted up his pillowcase and said, "Boo!"

The man yelled,

"Ahhhhhhhhhhhh!"

and fell right over.

But Lance wanted some candy so he said very softly, "Trick or treat!"

Nothing happened.

He said it a little louder: "Trick or treat!"

Nothing happened.

So Lance went inside and there was an enormous table full of candy.

He put it ALL in his bag:

KAAAAA-*THUMP!*

Then, even though his bag was very heavy, he walked down the street and went to another house:

KNOCK KNOCK KNOCK.

A lady opened up the door and said, "First kid for Halloween! So nice to see a little kid for Halloween."

Lance lifted up the pillowcase and said, "Boo!"

The lady yelled,

"Ahhhhhhhhhhhh!"

and fell right over.

But Lance wanted some candy so he said very softly, "Trick or treat!"

Nothing happened.

He said it a little louder: "Trick or treat!"

Nothing happened.

So Lance went inside and there was an enormous table full of candy. He put it ALL in his bag.

KAAAAA-*THUMP!*

Then Lance went into the kitchen and opened up the refrigerator. He took out ten boxes of ice cream, twenty cans of ginger ale, three watermelons, ten frozen pizzas, and a turkey.

Lance dragged the pillowcase across the porch. He fell down the stairs and landed in the middle of the street.

A police car came by. The policeman jumped out, looked at Lance and said, "Kid, what's the matter with you? You can't sit in the middle of the street. Take your candy and go home."

"Look," said Lance, "my bag is so heavy I can't even move. I live right down the street. Please carry my bag home."

"Well, all right," said the policeman. "I'll take your bag of candy to your house . . . WHOA! IT'S A HEAVY BAG OF CANDY!"

The policeman dragged the bag down the street, put it on Lance's front porch, and said, "Kid! You must have gone to two thousand houses to get so much candy!"

"No," said Lance, "just two."

"Wait a minute," said the policeman. "How did you get so much candy at just two houses?"

"Well," said Lance, "my face is so scary, when people see it they fall over and I take all the candy in the house."

"Hmm," said the policeman. "I'm a cop. You can't scare me. I want to see your face."

"OK," said Lance. He lifted up his pillowcase and said, "Boo!"

The policeman said, "Oh, if you think I'm going to fall over just because of a face like that, you are wrong. I'm going . . . I'm going . . . I'm going to . . . RUN AWAY!" And he jumped into his car and drove away really fast.

ZOOOOOOOOOOM!

Then Lance went inside and started to eat his first chocolate bar.

There was a knock on the door. Lance opened it and there was a teenager, the kind of kid who is much too old to go out for Halloween . . . and still goes out anyway!

He had a pillowcase over his head and a bag full of candy, much bigger than Lance's.

"Wow!" said Lance. "You must have gone to five thousand houses to get so much candy."

"No," said the teenager, "just five."

"How did you get so much candy at just five houses?" said Lance.

The teenager said, "My face is so scary that when people see it, they fall over, and I take all the candy in the house. And now I am going to scare *you* and take all the candy in *your* house."

"Maybe not!" said Lance. "I want to see your face."

"OK!" said the teenager. He lifted his pillowcase and yelled, "Boo!"

He had:

worms coming out of his hair,

butterflies coming out of his nose,

and ants coming out of his mouth.

He was scary, but not nearly as scary as Lance.

"Nice try," said Lance. He lifted his pillowcase and said,

The teenager yelled,

"Ahhhhhhhhhhhh!"

dropped his bag of candy, and ran down the street.

Lance took the teenager's bag of candy and dragged it into his house.

His candy lasted a long time. Every day, Lance ate as much as he could. He ate candy for breakfast, lunch, and dinner. He ate candy in the middle of the night. But his candy still lasted until . . .

BOO!

In June of 1991 I got a letter inviting me to visit the Grade 1/2 class at Lloyd George Public School in Hamilton, Ontario. I decided to drop in without telling anyone I was coming. The teacher freaked out when I walked in, but the kids thought it was neat.

While I was telling stories, a boy named Lance asked for a story about Halloween. He said that Halloween was his favourite day of the year. I made up a story for Lance that was sort of like the book, only it did not have the part with the teenager.

I told this story for a long time before it got good. When I finally decided to make it into a book, Lloyd George School was closed and I could not track down Lance. Happily, the teacher got in touch with me when she heard that I was looking for him. It turned out that Lance had moved back to Jamaica, but the teacher still had his picture.

Lloyd George School was right across the street from an enormous steel mill. The mill is the backdrop in some of the pictures.

— R.M.

*For Matthew Luttman,
Guelph, Ontario.*
— R.M.

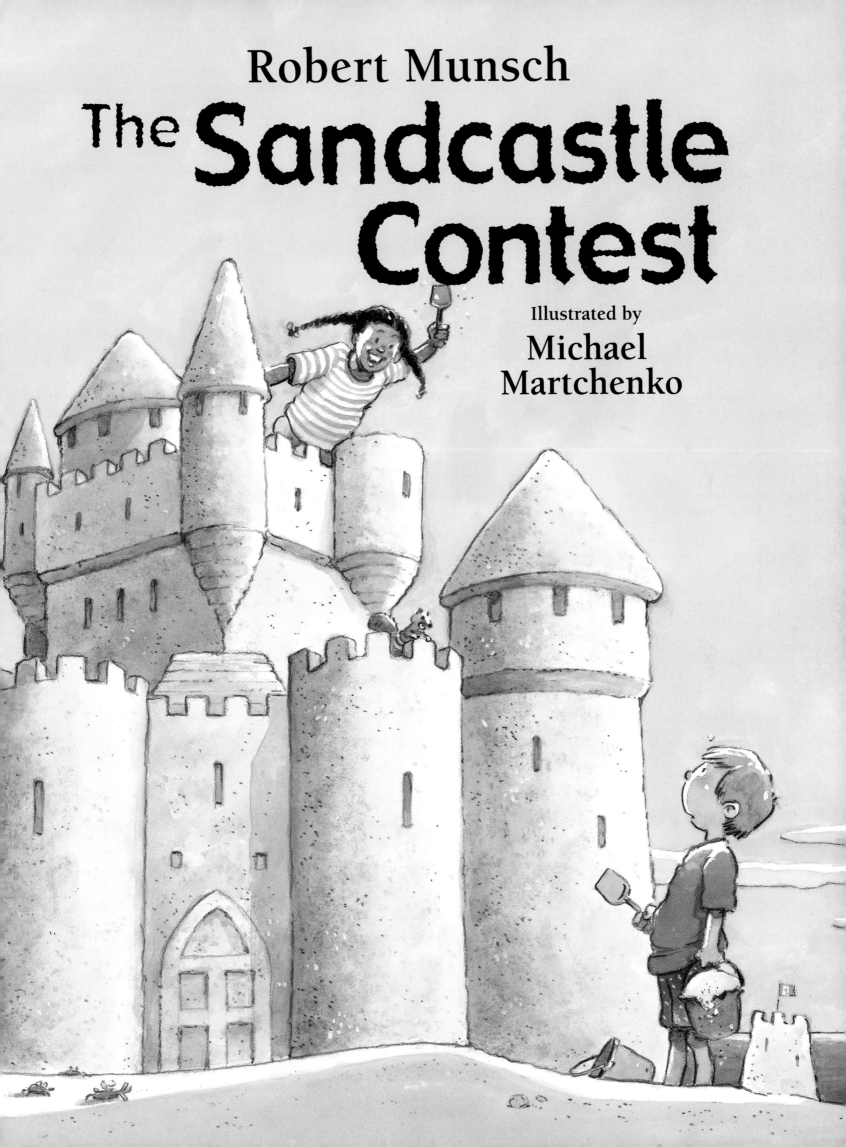

Robert Munsch
The Sandcastle Contest

Illustrated by
Michael Martchenko

Matthew's father stood in the driveway and said, "I think we are all ready to go! Let's make sure everything is here. Do we have the bicycles?"

"YES!"

"Do we have the food?"

"YES!"

"Do we have the boat?"

"YES!"

"Do we have everything?"

"NO!" yelled Matthew.

"No?" said his dad.

"No!" said Matthew. "We don't have a dog."

"Dog?" said his dad. "We don't even own a dog!"

"I know," said Matthew. "Now would be a good time to get a dog."

"No dog!" said his dad. "Now, do we have everything?"

"NO!" yelled Matthew. "We don't have my sandbox."

"Matthew," said his mom, "we can't bring the sandbox, but the first place we camp will have a nice beach, and you will have lots of sand to play with."

"Well," said Matthew, "OK."

So they drove and drove and drove and drove and drove, until they came to a place to camp.

Matthew jumped out of the van and ran to the beach.

He came to a girl making a small sandcastle and a big sand dog. She said, "Hi! My name is Kalita and I'm going to win the sandcastle contest!"

"Wow!" said Matthew. "I am going to build a sandcastle too. What can I win?"

"You can win a bathtub full of ice cream," said Kalita.

"All right!" said Matthew.

So Matthew made a
house with doors and
windows and a roof.
    He dug out the inside of
the house so it had rooms,
just like a real house.

He made sand tables and chairs and beds
and a TV that had a sand show on it.

When Matthew was almost done, Kalita came over to look at his house. She had her sand dog on a leash.

"Nice sand house," said Kalita.

"Really, really nice sand dog," said Matthew.

A judge came by and said, "Get this house out of here! Who put this house on the beach?"

"This is my sand house," said Matthew. "I made it for the sand contest."

"Ha!" said the judge. "I know a real house when I see one, and there are no real houses allowed on the beach!"

Then he went inside and sat in a sand chair and watched a sand show on TV.

Another judge came by and said, "Get this house out of here! Who put this house on the beach?"

"This is my sand house," said Matthew. "I made it for the sand contest."

"HA!" said the judge. "I know a real house when I see one, and there are no real houses allowed on the beach!"

She went into the bedroom and looked at the sand bed. She went into the kitchen, opened the refrigerator, and looked at the sand apples and the sand celery and the sand cartons of milk. Then she said, "Little boy, you've got to get this house off the beach."

"This is my sand house," said Matthew, "and I am going to prove it."

"HA!" said the judges.

So Matthew went outside and kicked the sand house right beside the door. It all turned back into an enormous pile of sand and fell on the judges.

"HELP!" yelled the judges, and everyone came running and dug them out.

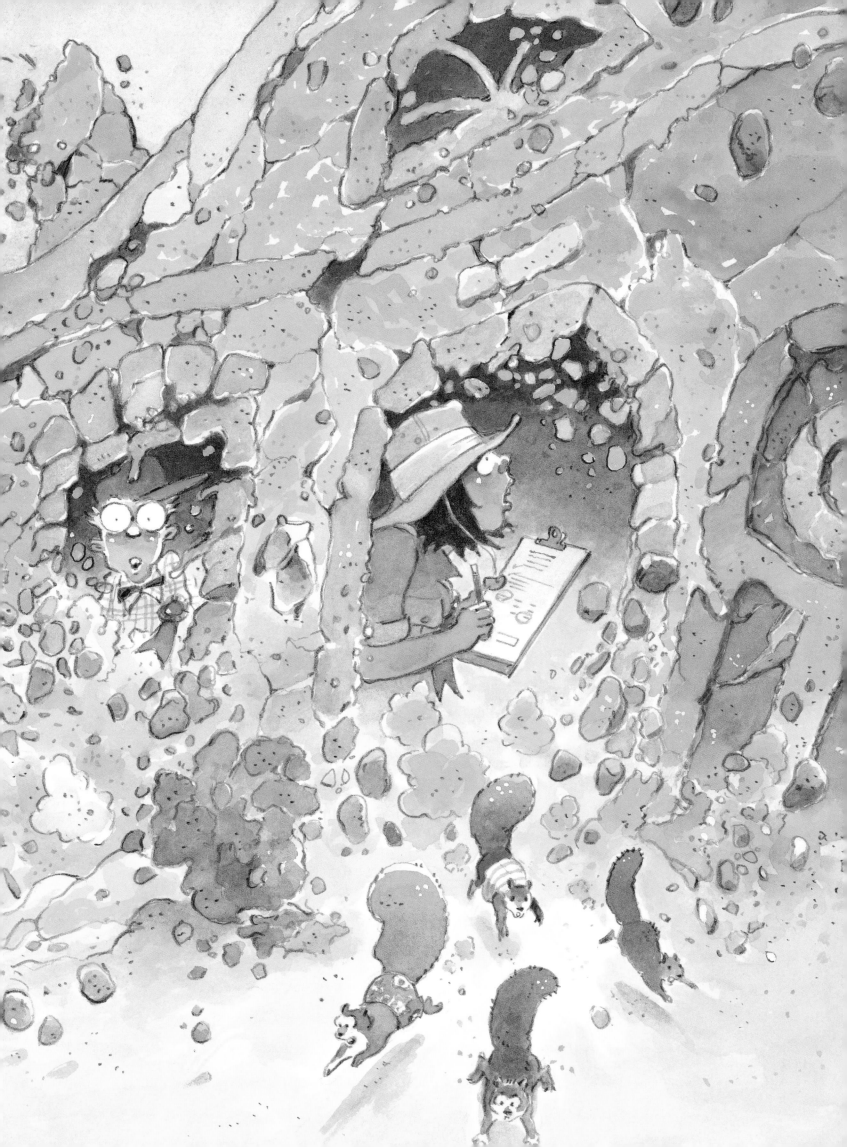

When the judges were finally out from under the sand, they yelled, "Matthew wins! His sand house was so good that we thought it was a real house."

"Matthew wins!" everyone yelled, and they gave him a bathtub full of ice cream.

Matthew started eating the ice cream and he said to Kalita, "Want to help me eat this?"

"Yes," said Kalita.

While they were eating the ice cream Matthew said, "How come you didn't tell everybody that your dog is sand? I bet you would have won with a sand dog."

"Well," said Kalita, "this is Sandy, my sand dog, and I am going to take him camping and feed him ice cream every day and he is going to be my pet and I am never going to turn him back to sand."

"WOW!" said Matthew. "I wish I had thought of that. Can you show me how to make one?"

"No problem," said Kalita.

And Matthew's mom and dad were
so happy with Matthew's amazing sand
dog that . . .

they decided to
take it camping.

The Sandcastle Contest

The Sandcastle Contest is three stories that got stuck together. One story was made up in 1992 for my daughter, Tyya, while we were on vacation on a little island in the Caribbean called Nevis. Tyya was six years old then, and she loved to build sandcastles. I made up a story where she built such a nice sandcastle that everybody thought it was a real castle. This story became one of my beach stories, and I told it whenever I was telling stories on a beach or a sandbox.

Meanwhile, every summer the Luttmans, who live on my street, loaded up a camper with all sorts of stuff and then put five bicycles on top of the camper and drove off. I decided to make up a story about a family who took along EVERYTHING for a camping trip.

Meanwhile, I knew the Luttman kids were bugging their parents to get a dog. I had made up lots of stories about kids who wanted a dog, but none of them was ever any good.

All of a sudden, these three things all got tangled into one story, and out came *The Sandcastle Contest*.

— R.M.

157

*Dedicated to the children
at Bukati Primary School,
Butula, Kenya.*

Braids

Written by

Robert Munsch

illustrated by
The children of Sir Isaac Brock Public School

On Saturday, when Ashley was sitting at the breakfast table, her mother came in and said, "Look at your hair. It's a mess! It needs a few braids before you go out and play."

"A few!" yelled Ashley. "You always put in a million braids and you pull on my hair and it hurts and it takes all day! I never do anything but get my hair braided.

"NO! NO! NO!"

Then Ashley ran around the breakfast table screaming

"Ahhhh! Ahhhh! Ahhhh! Ahhhh!"

while her mother tried to catch her.

After they had gone around the breakfast table seventeen times, Ashley's mother caught Ashley, sat her on a chair and started to braid her hair.

It took an hour because Ashley's mom
braided her hair
back and forth
and
back and forth
and
back and forth,
AND
        up and down
        and
        up and down
        and
        up and down,
        AND
                round and round and
                round and round and
                round and round.

When she was done, Ashley looked in the mirror and said,

"Oh, look!

"It's beautiful.

"It's wonderful.

"But it took forever!

"I wish you didn't like to braid my hair."

Then Ashley went outside and sat down on the front steps of her house and was unhappy.

People came by and said, "Hey, Ashley! Nice hair," and Ashley didn't say anything.

Then Ashley's grandmother came by and said "Ashley! What wonderful braids. But why are you so mad?"

"It's that mother of mine!" said
Ashley. "She likes to braid my hair. It
takes all day and I never do anything
but get my hair braided. Some kids
go to the mall, some kids play games,
I just get my hair braided."

"It looks very nice," said her
grandmother.

"I don't like it," said Ashley.

"Do you know," said her grandmother,
"why your mother likes to braid like that?"

"No," said Ashley. "She learned it from me," said her grandmother. "When your mommy was a little girl I used to braid her hair all the time. It took all day."

"How come you don't braid her hair now?" said Ashley.

"Can't catch her," said her grandmother.

"Maybe both of us could catch her!" said Ashley.

"Good idea," said her grandmother.

So Ashley and her grandmother walked into the house and Ashley's grandmother said to Ashley's mother, "Look at your hair. It needs some BRAIDS!"

"NO, NO, NO!" yelled Ashley's mom. "I am grown up now and you can't do that stuff with me anymore. NO! NO! NO! NO!"

Ashley's grandmother said, "Now
come on, Sweet Pea, I'm going to braid
your hair."

Ashley's mom ran around the
breakfast table screaming
"AHHHH! AHHHH! AHHHH! AHHHH!"
while Ashley and her grandmother
tried to catch her.

They chased Ashley's mother around the table seventeen times until they finally caught her. Then they sat her in a chair and braided her hair for two hours.

It took two hours because they braided the hair

back and forth
and
back and forth
and
back and forth,
AND   up and down
                       and
                       up and down
                       and
                       up and down,
                       AND   round and round and
                                    round and round and
                                    round and round.

When they were done, Ashley's
mother looked in the mirror and said,
   "Oh look!
   "It's beautiful.
   "It's wonderful.
   "But it took forever.
   "I wish you didn't like to braid my
hair."

Then Ashley and her mother sat out on
the front step and were both unhappy.

Ashley's teacher came by and said "My!
What lovely braids. I wish I had hair like that."

"Let's get her!" said Ashley.

"Get who?" said the teacher.

"GET YOU!" said Ashley. "We're going
to braid your hair and it will take all day!"

"AHHHHHHHHHHHHHHHHH!"
yelled the teacher. She ran down the
street, and Ashley and her mom and her
grandmother and all the neighbours ran
after her. They chased the teacher around
the block seventeen times until Ashley
finally caught her.

Then they sat her on a mailbox and
braided her hair.

It took six hours because they braided it

back and forth
and
back and forth
and
back and forth,
AND

up and down
and
up and down
and
up and down,
AND

round and round and
round and round and
round and round.

When they were done the teacher had
a thousand little braids in her hair. She
looked sort of like a porcupine.

"Looks nice!" said Ashley's
grandmother.

"Looks great!" said Ashley's mother.

"Wow!" said Ashley's teacher. "I'm
going to wear these braids to school!"

And Ashley decided not to tell her
teacher that sometimes people just do
not look good in braids.

Braids

At the end of a storytelling at the Guelph Public Library in 2009, Taya Kendall came up to me and said that she was putting out a school newspaper. Not bad for someone in Grade Three. She wanted to know if she could put one of my stories in her newspaper. I suggested that she use "Braids," which I had told with her name in it at the library. I often give unpublished stories to kids, and that is that.

Well, not only did she use it in the newspaper, she published it as a book, with artwork by a different kid for each page — all students at Sir Isaac Brock Public School — including her six-year-old sister Eden. Not bad for someone in Grade Three.

Taya sold the book as as a fundraiser for a charity called Children of Bukati, which supports orphans and poor children in the rural village of Butula, Kenya, and their school, Bukati Primary School. Taya has raised thousands of dollars for the children of Bukati. Not bad for someone in Grade Three!

Publisher's note: Scholastic Canada has made a donation to Children of Bukati in the name of the students of Sir Isaac Brock School.

Robert Munsch is Canada's best-selling children's book author, and no wonder – his books include such classics as *The Paper Bag Princess*, *Love You Forever*, and *We Share Everything!* Robert developed his storytelling skill when he was working in daycare and needed to settle the kids down. Now he tells stories to thousands at a time, and his books are published in more than twenty languages and enjoyed around the world.

Although the stories come from Robert's wild imagination, they always begin with a real kid — someone he knows, someone who writes to him, or kids who put their hands up at storytellings. Then he tells the stories over and over until they are perfect. Sometimes the kids are grown up by the time the books are actually published!

Robert lives in Guelph, Ontario with his family and two dogs: a very large poodle and a very small Yorkshire terrier. In 2009, he was honoured with a star on Canada's Walk of Fame.

Michael Martchenko has been an artist for as long as he can remember. As a boy he copied comic books; after high school he went to the Ontario College of Art and worked for several years at an advertising agency. Then one of his paintings caught the eye of Robert Munsch and his publisher. That led to the very first Munsch-Martchenko collaboration, *The Paper Bag Princess*. Now, more than 40 books later, they are the most popular picture-book team in the country.

Michael brings his own crazy sense of humour to the books and always includes jokes in the illustrations, along with images of his other books and characters, and his trademark pterodactyl. But Michael doesn't just illustrate Robert Munsch stories. He's created many other successful books, some of which he also wrote. When he is not creating books, he plays the guitar, walks his Cairn terrier, Mindy, and paints aviation art. He lives in Toronto, Ontario.

Thanks to the students of Sir Isaac Brock Public School in Guelph, Ontario, who contributed to the illustrations for *Braids*. We are sorry that we didn't have space to use every single piece of the beautiful art you created!

Iman A, page 174; Shahana A, page 163 (top); Gabby B, page 180 (top left); James B, page 161 (top); Sarina B, page 163 (bottom); Madelyn C, page 161 (bottom); Sarah D, page 165; Tyler D, page 177; Jakob G, page 180 (bottom right); Kylee G, page 162; Sukhraj G, page 169; Kaitlin H, page 164; Kara H, page 168 (bottom); Scott H, page 166 (top); Tyler H, page 168 (top); Aislynn J, page 166 (bottom); Eden K, page 160; Taya K, pages 159, 175; Karina L, page 158 (bottom); Ann Glory M, page 167; Lauren M, page 171; Cameron P, page 180 (top right); Jessica P, page 176; Naomi P, page 173; Alison T, page 172; Lazar V, page 170 (top); Owen VRP, page 158 (top); Madison W, page 170 (bottom); Ellen Z, page 180 (bottom left).

With special thanks to Rebecca Kendall for all her help.